KARNER'S QUEST
∼ for Blue Lupine ∼

AUTHOR
Sara Jo Dickens, PhD

ILLUSTRATED BY
Nancy Scheibe

Enjoy!
Nancy Scheibe
Thank you again!

ISBN 13: 978-1-59298-923-2

Library of Congress Catalog Number: 2014910065

Printed in the United States of America

First Printing: 2014

18 17 16 15 14   5 4 3 2 1

BEAVER'S POND
PRESS

7108 Ohms Lane
Edina, MN 55439-2129
(952) 829-8818
www.BeaversPondPress.com

To order, visit www.BeaversPondBooks.com
Or call (800) 901-3480. Reseller discounts available.

To my nieces and nephews,

Payton, Parker, Delaine, Antonio, Grayson and Alexis. May nature always provide you a place to seek adventure and discover yourselves.

Anna Marie watches the warm sun melt
the winter snow in her garden,
and in the forest just beyond her yard.

Leaf buds form on the oaks,
and the pines sprout new shoots.
Already she sees bright white trillium
and twinflowers blooming outside.
Her favorite time of year
is finally here—spring.

SOON THE BUTTERFLIES
WILL ARRIVE!

Every spring Anna Marie paints the butterflies
that gather and dance, collecting pollen and
nectar from her garden. She loves to fill her
pictures with splashes of green, orange, red,
and her favorite color, blue.

But before the butterflies will come,
their favorite flowers must grow.

One special day each year,
Anna Marie and her mom
go to the nursery to buy
flowers for the garden.

TODAY IS THAT DAY.

"Which plants do butterflies like best?"
  asks Anna Marie.
"Well, butterflies love many flowers,"
  says the nursery worker,
"but if you want even more butterflies,
  let me show you which flowers
  will feed their caterpillars."

"Plant me in your garden,"
  calls the pink milkweed,
"and the monarchs will come."
"Me, me, me!" calls the black-eyed Susan,
"Swallowtail caterpillars love me!"

"Take me home," calls the sunflower,
"if you'd like to meet some checkerspots."
"I'll bring lots of buckeyes!"
  calls the snapdragon.

Soon Anna Marie's mom's truck
  is filled so full of flowers that
  there's hardly room to sit!

Anna Marie carefully helps plant marigolds,
pink milkweed, coneflowers, sunflowers,
black-eyed Susans, purple garden lupine,
red penstemon, roses, and more.

"Mom, how long before the butterflies come?"
"Soon, sweetheart, you need to be patient."

Then one day she sees a tiger swallowtail
resting on a sunflower.

"Your paintings are so bright. Will you paint one of me?"
asks the tiger swallowtail. Anna Marie giggles with
delight as the butterfly stretches to show off his
blue-spotted yellow and black wings.

Soon monarchs, sulphurs, and checkerspots
swirl and dance around the blossoms.

ANNA MARIE PAINTS THEM ALL.

As the sun goes down,
her mom comes looking for her.
"Come in, it's time for dinner!"

"I can't go in, one isn't here yet."
"Which one?" asks Mom.

Anna Marie holds up a picture
she'd painted last summer.
"I'm waiting for the Karner blue."
"Beautiful," says Mom,
"but you need to come in and eat.
The butterflies have all gone home to sleep."

As soon as the sun rises the next morning,
Anna Marie jumps out of bed and runs barefoot
through cool, dewy grass to the garden.

She examines the orange lilies and buries her nose
deep into the red and white roses. She wanders
through the garden enjoying the aromas.

THEN SHE SEES IT—

Wings of blue!
But something is wrong.

Why is the butterfly on the ground?
Why isn't he flying?

The blue butterfly looks tired,
and he's holding something
in his front legs.

"Hello, my name is Anna Marie."

"I'm Karner," he replies, in a shaky voice,
"and this is Melissa." She can see that
he's holding a tiny caterpillar.

"You don't look so well, Karner."

"I'm tired," he says, "and my little
sister is hungry. I took her out for a
fly to explore, but now I don't have the
strength to get her back home."

"There are so many plants in my garden.
Let me bring you to your favorite,
for your little sister to eat."

"Thank you," says Karner, "but Melissa can't eat the leaves of these flowers." Anna Marie is confused. "Why not? I planted these for the butterflies."

"Do you eat fruits and vegetables?" he asks. "Yes, I do. I love blueberries, especially in muffins."

"Would you eat a pinecone?" asks Karner. "No—that's not people food. It would hurt my mouth and give me a tummy ache."

"Well, these flowers are like pinecones to Melissa. They're not good for Karner blue caterpillars," he explains. "They'd make Melissa's tummy ache, and they wouldn't taste good either. She needs the leaves of one special flower. I thought I'd find some near here but it seems they only grow in the forest now. Our family is getting bigger and soon there may not be enough for us all."

"I know! I'll carry you back to your home." Anna Marie carefully lowers her hands to the ground, and Karner climbs into them with Melissa snuggled in close.

"Mom, can I take a walk in the forest?" she calls.

"Yes, dear," replies her mom, pulling up weeds, "but be home before lunch!"

Anna Marie bravely walks out of her yard and into the forest.

It's darker and cooler in the forest.

Tiny goose bumps pop up on her bare arms.
"Don't worry," says Karner. "Soon we'll be
out of the trees and it will be warmer."

After passing through many oaks and pines,
they reach a sunny clearing filled with
beautiful flowers of purple and blue.

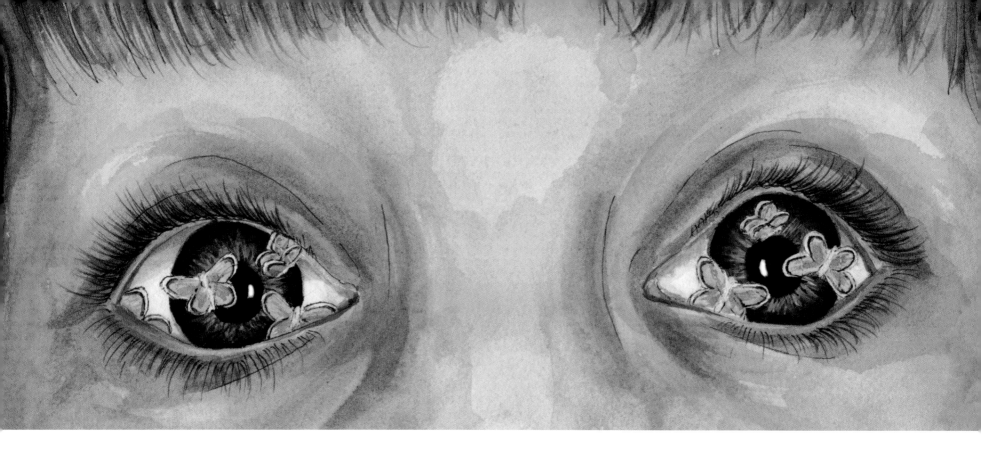

Her eyes widen in wonder to see that the clearing is
also filled with butterflies, flitting and chasing each
other from flower to flower, and each one with a
question for Karner!

"Where have you been?" "Do you have Melissa?"
"What did you see?" "Who is your friend?"
"Were you scared?"

"Yes, very scared!" replies Karner.

"You don't need to be scared anymore,"
says Anna Marie, with a warm smile.

While Karner explains how Anna Marie
rescued them, she carefully sets Melissa
on the long, slender leaf of a flower.
The caterpillar burrows into the carpet of
hairs covering the leaf and begins to eat.

Anna Marie realizes that this special flower,
like all of the others in the clearing, is a lupine.

"I don't understand," she cries.
"I planted flowers like this.
  Why won't you all come to my
  garden? I planted lots of lupine!"

"Don't be upset, sweet child,"
  says the flower holding Melissa.
"There's more than one kind of lupine."

"I'm the wild blue lupine, called perennes.
You planted polyphyllus, my cousin,
also known as 'garden lupine.'

Her leaves are pointier than mine, and her
flowers are taller and come in many colors.
My flowers are only purple, or blue with white.
But most importantly, her leaves aren't good for
Karner blue caterpillars. Karner blue caterpillars
need wild blue lupine."

"Why don't you live closer to my house?"
asks Anna Marie.

"That, my dear, is a very wise question,"
perennes replies.

"Long ago, wild blue lupine lived in oak savannas
and pine barrens all over eastern North America,
but most of those trees have been cut down to
make room for people, and now there are so many
other plants that there isn't much room for us.

So we live in smaller areas where healthy oak
savannas and pine barrens can still be found."

Anna Marie is sad to hear this.

"Would you like to help me and the butterflies?"
    perennes asks.

"Yes," says Anna Marie, wiping away a tear,
"I'd love to help the Karner blue caterpillars."

"Cheer up, sweet girl, and give me your hand."
    Perennes drops large dark seeds into her palm.
"If you plant these in your garden, Karner blue
    butterflies will come."

"Oh, thank you! May I come back
for more seeds next spring?"

"No need," says perennes.
"We're perennial plants.
We bloom in the warm months
and then go to sleep in the
autumn to escape the winter cold.
As soon as the sun melts the snow,
we awaken and bloom each spring."

Anna Marie is happy again.
"I promise to care for these plants
year after year."

She clutches the seeds tightly
in her hands so she won't lose
them on her way home.

With a good-bye to her new friends,
she runs back through the forest
and straight to her garden to plant
the wild blue lupine seeds.

Every day Anna Marie checks on the seeds, which soon become seedlings.

First, fat dark leaves emerge from the dirt. Next come several stems upon which skinny, fan-shaped leaves unfold.

Before long, the stems are covered with buds that look like small ears of corn.

Finally, they blossom into tiny blue and white flowers, just like perennes.

Anna Marie loves the flowers so much,
she decides to paint them.

But before she can pick up her brush,
she sees little sparkles of blue in the air.

Soon she's encircled by a dancing
cloud of blue wings.

"Karner!" she yells, jumping to her feet.
Karner and his friends swirl all around
her and land on the wild blue lupine.

One teeny, tiny butterfly lands on her fingertip.

"Remember me?" she asks in a soft, shy voice.

"Melissa!" gasps Anna Marie,
"You've changed so much!"
"So has your garden."

"I planted these flowers just for you."

26

Karner lands on a nearby lupine.

"Thank you, Anna Marie. Now we can play in your garden every year."

AND THEY DO.

The Plight of the Karner Blue Butterfly

Karner blue butterflies were once common from Minnesota to the East Coast, and south through Ohio and Indiana. This small butterfly is only one inch wide, and has lost 75 percent of its original habitat. It was listed as an endangered species in 1992.

—*Actual Size*

Adult Karners will feed on the nectar of most native flowers, but the Karner caterpillars can only eat the leaves of the wild blue lupine. This flower grows best in oak savannas and pine barrens. Oak savannas are open grasslands with one or more oak trees. They used to be one of the most common habitats in the Midwestern United States. Pine barrens are made up of a mixture of grasses, shrubs, low trees, and a few tall pines. Most of these habitats have been replaced by buildings, roads, or other human land uses, which means that Karner blue caterpillars can no longer find food.

How Can You Help?

The best way to help the Karner, if you live in the Midwestern United States, is to bring its food source into your gardens and neighborhoods. By planting this blue, purple, and white native, you increase the possible range of the Karner. However, not all lupine are equal. What's widely called 'lupine' is actually several different species, and Karner blue caterpillars can only eat the native wild blue lupine, whose scientific name is Lupinus perennes. The most commonly sold lupine is a horticultural non-native, whose name is Lupinus polyphyllus, and this won't feed the Karner caterpillar.

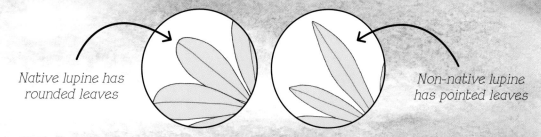

Native lupine has rounded leaves　　　*Non-native lupine has pointed leaves*

It's fairly easy to tell the native lupine plant from the non-natives. The native lupine has rounded leaf ends, but non-native lupines have pointed leaf ends. The native lupine also produces only flowers colored half blue-purple and half white. If your lupine has flowers of any other color, it's not the native.

For more information on how you can help preserve the Karner blue butterfly and the native, wild blue lupine, contact your local Department of Fish and Wildlife, the Nature Conservancy or the US Fish and Wildlife offices. Every action, no matter how small, helps to keep our forests full of the wildlife and plants that make them so special.

REFERENCES:
· Dirig, R. 1973. "The Endangered Karner Blue." The Conservationist. October-November, pp. 6, 47.

· Grundel, R., N.B. Pavlovic and C.L. Sulzman. "Habitat use by the endangered Karner blue butterfly in oak woodlands: the influence of canopy cover."

· Ritter, D. (ed.). 1976. "Karner's famous blue butterfly." In Pine Bush: · Albany's Last Frontier. Pine Bush Historic Preservation Project, pp. 197-210.

· Stewart, M. M. and C. Ricci. 1988. "Dearth of the Blues." Natural History. May. pp. 64-71.

Help Karner Find His Forest Friends

Friend Key

Angleworm	*Ant*	*Blue Jay*	*Bumble Bee*
Cardinal	*Caterpillar*	*Chipmunk*	*Chickadee*
Compton Tortoiseshell	*Dragonfly*	*Frog*	*Grasshopper*
Karner Blue Butterfly	*Karner Blue Caterpilar*	*Ladybug*	*Monarch*
Turtle	*Mouse*	*Nuthatch*	*Owl*
Rabbit	*Robin*	*Spider*	*Sparrow*
Squirrel	*Tiger Swallowtail*	*Toad*	

Find Karner's Friends

Cover	1 Chipmunk, 1 Karner Blue Butterfly, 4 Karner Blue Butterfly Caterpillars
Pg. 4	1 Chickadee, 1 Dragonfly
Pg. 5	1 Chipmunk, 1 Robin, 1 Dragonfly
Pg. 6	1 Compton Tortoiseshell Butterfly, 1 Dragonfly, 1 Sparrow, 1 Turtle, 1 Tiger Swallowtail Butterfly
Pg. 7	1 Dragonfly, 2 Mice
Pg. 8	1 Angleworm, 1 Dragonfly, 1 Frog
Pg. 9	1 Dragonfly, 1 Monarch Butterfly, 1 Tiger Swallow Butterfly
Pg. 10	1 Dragonfly, 1 Grasshopper
Pg. 11	1 Dragonfly, 1 Ladybug, 1 Toad
Pg. 12	3 Bumble Bees, 1 Dragonfly, 1 Karner Blue Butterfly, 1 Karner Blue Butterfly Caterpillar
Pg. 13	1 Ant, 1 Dragonfly, 1 Karner Blue Butterfly, 1 Karner Blue Butterfly Caterpillar, 1 Ladybug
Pg. 14	1 Angleworm, 1 Blue Jay, 1 Dragonfly, 1 Karner Blue Butterfly
Pg. 15	2 Dragonflies, 1 Frog, 1 Karner Blue Butterfly, 1 Karner Blue Butterfly Caterpillar
Pg. 16	1 Dragonfly, 1 Karner Blue Butterfly, 1 Owl
Pg. 17	1 Cardinal, 1 Dragonfly, 17 Karner Blue Butterflies, 1 Rabbit, 1 Turtle
Pg. 19	1 Caterpillar, 1 Dragonfly, 1 Karner Blue Butterfly, 1 Karner Blue Caterpillar, 1 Squirrel, 1 Ladybug
Pg. 20	1 Bumble Bee, 1 Dragonfly, 12 Karner Blue Butterflies
Pg. 21	1 Dragonfly
Pg. 22	1 Chipmunk, 1 Dragonfly, 1 Karner Blue Butterfly, 1 Spider
Pg. 23	1 Dragonfly, 2 Nuthatches, 1 Rabbit, 1 Turtle
Pg. 24	1 Angleworm, 2 Ants, 1 Dragonfly, 1 Ladybug
Pg. 25	1 Chipmunk, 1 Dragonfly, 56 Karner Blue Butterflies, 1 Robin
Pg. 26	1 Dragonfly, 1 Karner Blue Butterfly
Pg. 27	8 Karner Blue Butterflies

Glossary

Aroma- A scent or smell.

Dew- Water droplets that cover the ground on summer mornings.

Endangered Species- A species that has been legally listed by the federal government as having a population size so small it is at risk of going extinct.

Habitat- A type of place that a particular plant or animal lives because the environment provides what the plant or animal needs to live.

Native- Any species of plant or animal that naturally belongs in an area, and wasn't introduced by humans. Also known as indigenous.

Non-native- Plants and animals that were introduced to an area by humans either on purpose or by accident. Also sometimes called introduced species, alien, or exotic.

Nectar- A sweet, sugary liquid that flowers make and insects and birds eat. Flowers make nectar to attract insects that will unknowingly carry the flower's pollen to other flowers.

Perennial Plant- A plant that lives for more than two years. If it dies by winter, it can return in the spring or summer.

Pollen- A powder-like material within the flower that fertilizes female flowers or flower parts, allowing the flowers to produce fruit.

Seedling- A young plant that grows from a seed. (Not all plants are grown from seeds; some can be grown from cuttings of other plants, bulbs or root fragments.)

Author
Sara Jo Dickens, PhD

Sara Jo is a native of Minnesota where she spent many childhood hours in the woods. Currently, she resides in Park City, Utah with her husband and two dogs, Saydi and Stella. She believes that nature plays a crucial role in healthy childhood development, and that conservation of wildlands, for centuries to come, depends on establishing a connection with nature at childhood. Sara Jo works as an ecological scientist with the University of California, Berkeley aiding in development of more effective wildland restoration strategies.

Artist
Nancy Scheibe

Nancy is Sara Jo's mother. She likes the challenge of working in several different mediums, including snow in the winter. Nancy is primarily self taught. Her work is a mix of classical, abstract, impressionistic, and whimsical. She is also an author of three books about a kayak adventure she took down the Mississippi River. She lives in Ely, Minnesota with her husband, Doug, their dog, Carly, and cat, Simon. To see more of Nancy's work go to www.NancyScheibe.com.

Model for Anna Marie
Sveltana Leplatt

Svetlana loves animals and is looking forward to enjoying this book with kids! She lives in Chanhassen, Minnesota where she has a puppy named Lovey, one cat named Barney, and a crayfish. In the summer Svetlana lives in Ely, Minnesota.

ACKNOWLEDGMENTS
Meg Heimann, our editor, Judd Salvas, our graphic design artist, and many family and friends who acted as sounding boards for ideas and improvements.